SNOWPEA
THE PUPPY QUEEN

KITTEN LADY

HANNAH SHAW

Adventures in FOSTERLAND

Illustrated by
BEV JOHNSON

SNOWPEA THE PUPPY QUEEN

Aladdin

New York   London   Toronto   Sydney   New Delhi

This book is a work of fiction. Any references to historical events, real people, or real places are used fictitiously. Other names, characters, places, and events are products of the author's imagination, and any resemblance to actual events or places or persons, living or dead, is entirely coincidental.

ALADDIN

An imprint of Simon & Schuster Children's Publishing Division
1230 Avenue of the Americas, New York, New York 10020
First Aladdin paperback edition July 2023
Copyright © 2023 by Kitten Lady, LLC.
Also available in an Aladdin hardcover edition.
All rights reserved, including the right of reproduction in whole or in part in any form.
ALADDIN and related logo are registered trademarks of Simon & Schuster, Inc.
For information about special discounts for bulk purchases, please contact
Simon & Schuster Special Sales at 1-866-506-1949
or business@simonandschuster.com.
The Simon & Schuster Speakers Bureau can bring authors to your live event. For
more information or to book an event contact the Simon & Schuster
Speakers Bureau at 1-866-248-3049 or visit our website
at www.simonspeakers.com.
Designed by Tiara Iandiorio
The illustrations for this book were rendered digitally.
The text of this book was set in Banda.
Manufactured in the United States of America 0623 OFF
2 4 6 8 10 9 7 5 3 1
Library of Congress Cataloging-in-Publication Data
Names: Shaw, Hannah René, 1987- author. | Johnson, Bev, illustrator.
Title: Snowpea the puppy queen / by Hannah Shaw ; illustrated by Bev Johnson.
Description: First Aladdin paperback edition. | New York : Aladdin, 2023. |
Series: Adventures in Fosterland | Summary: Snowpea teaches two boisterous
puppies how to behave properly in Fosterland.
Identifiers: LCCN 2023005825 (print) | LCCN 2023005826 (ebook) |
ISBN 9781665925587 (pbk) | ISBN 9781665925594 (hc) | ISBN 9781665925600 (ebook)
Subjects: CYAC: Cats—Fiction. | Dogs—Fiction. | Animals—Infancy—Fiction. | Behavior—
Fiction. | Foster home care—Fiction. | LCGFT: Animal fiction.
Classification: LCC PZ7.1.S4935 Sn 2023 (print) | LCC PZ7.1.S4935 (ebook) |
DDC [Fic]—dc23
LC record available at https://lccn.loc.gov/2023005825
LC ebook record available at https://lccn.loc.gov/2023005826

For every perfectly imperfect
person, puppy, and kitten
embracing life's messiness

Contents

CHAPTER 1

Perfectly Perfect

Snowpea's bedroom was spotless. The cat beds were freshly fluffed, and all the little toys were tucked away neatly into the toy bin. Not so much as a speck of litter was out of place.

Snowpea, a small white kitten with soft stripes and icy blue eyes, walked daintily along the edge of the window-sill, dusting it with her tail. "A clean home is a happy home!" she said, pausing to glimpse her reflection in the glass. She licked her pink paw pad and ran it through her fur. "And a clean cat is a happy cat!"

Next, Snowpea checked on her potted plants, rotating the cat mint to give it even sunlight, then tapped her paw into a dish of water and shook it to spritz the leaves.

With her plants tended to and everything looking just the way she liked it, Snowpea hopped down and pranced through the center of the room, which was lined on either side with tall scratch posts shaped like palm trees and sunflowers. It was a bright and cheery path that led to the tallest tower in the room: a cat castle where she liked to rest in the sunshine and enjoy the silence. She leapt to the tippy-top and gazed over her flawless, peaceful territory.

Life hadn't always been so perfect. Snowpea was born on the street, where all she knew was the horrible crunch of dirt between her toe beans and the sound of horns blaring on the highway. Back then, she didn't have a single thing to call her own, and she would cry out to the people passing by, longing for a chance at a fresh start. Luckily for her, a fairy godmother had scooped her up, dusted the filth from her fur, and brought her to Fosterland—a temporary residence where she could clean up and prepare for a forever home.

A forever home! The thought alone made her feel warm and fuzzy inside. *Who'd have thought a crusty little kitten like me could one day be adopted?* Sitting on top of her castle, she daydreamed about her future life as the ruler of her very own kingdom. Would she be a dignified duchess, demanding pets? Or a peaceful princess, purring on a lap?

At least in Fosterland, she could get plenty of practice being pampered!

One of the best things about being

a foster kitten, it seemed, was that she was showered with gifts. Each day, her fairy godmother would bring her something new and exciting to play with! As the door creaked open and the yellow-haired godmother approached, Snowpea leapt up, asking, "What do you have for me today?"

On this day, the fairy godmother pulled out a glittering wand, which sparkled in her hand. She waved the wand over Snowpea's head, and the way the light flickered upon it was enchanting. Snowpea squealed with delight as she reached for it again and again, tapping it with her paws until she finally grabbed the wand and pulled it

onto the castle top with her. As the godmother exited the room, Snowpea held the wand at her side like it was a royal scepter.

"Hear ye, hear ye! I am Queen Snowpea!" she called out. "Queen Snowpea," she repeated under her breath. "I like the sound of that."

"Looking quite regal up there," called a voice from the doorway.

It was Haroun, a big brown cat with a leopard-spotted coat. She knew him as one of the rulers of the Three-Cat Kingdom, the land just beyond the foster-room door. There, he lived with Coco and Eloise: wise, full-grown felines with shining coats and complete reign over their home and humans. Snowpea aspired to be as royal as them! She sat tall atop the tower, holding her wand at her side, trying to impress her visitor.

"Just don't take

yourself too seriously!" He smirked.

"But ruling over a territory *is* serious business," Snowpea said. "This is important practice for when I become the queen of a *real* kingdom someday— as all cats ought to do!"

"Indeed, Your Highness," Haroun joked.

"Which is precisely why everything has to be perfectly perfect! That's what forever families want in a cat, after all!"

Haroun looked at her with soft, wise eyes. "Just remember: No one is perfect. Not you, not the cats you might share your home with in the future, and not even me!"

Snowpea scrunched up her face.

It had never occurred to her that she might someday have to share her king-dom with others.

Haroun took a deep breath and spoke softly:

"You don't have to be pristine
To be a cherished, worthy queen.
Someday soon you'll come to see
It's love that makes us royalty.
Just be yourself, and do your best;
Embrace the real, embrace the mess.

**Love others for their charms
and flaws,
And they'll love you—with
open paws."**

Snowpea listened carefully, but when Haroun finished, she said, "Thanks, but you lost me at 'mess.' A queen doesn't do mess! As far as I can tell, I'm the only foster in Fosterland, and I like it that way. Besides, you know, everything must be orderly if I want to protect my territory against . . . you-know-who."

CHAPTER 2

You-Know-Who

Vrrrrrr . . .

As if she'd summoned him from across the land, Snowpea heard her mortal enemy rolling toward her room. It was the one and only thing that could threaten her happiness in Fosterland, and it was quickly approaching.

Vrrrrrr . . .

Startled, Haroun ran off, and

Snowpea shot straight into the air. Louder than the cars that used to speed past her on the highway, this was the sound of a terrifying beast.

"THE EVIL ROBOT MONSTER!" she screamed, her pupils widening like big black saucers.

VRRRR!

Her fur stood on end as her nemesis slid into the room. It was a dark circle-shaped monster that banged into the walls, bumped into scratch posts, and wreaked devastation by suctioning everything in its path through its teeth. All that it touched would be swallowed deep into an inner chamber, where it would never be seen again.

Snowpea's eyes darted around the room to search for any misplaced toys, but everything was exactly where it belonged.

"You won't steal from me today!" she hissed.

Snowpea remembered the first day she'd seen the monster. She was brand new to Fosterland, and she'd just been given her very first toy: a beautiful sparkle-mouse that made her leap through the air with glee! But then the monster had barged into her room, made a beeline for her sparkle-mouse— and swallowed it whole.

She could still feel a lump in her throat as she remembered watching

the little ribbon tail vanishing into the robot's teeth. It had stolen the first nice thing she'd ever had.

She vowed that day never to forgive it or to leave a single toy within its reach.

"There's nothing for you here, and there never will be! Now—be gone!" she growled over the whirring sound, holding her wand tightly between her trembling paws. She didn't want it to take away anything else she cared about!

The robot bopped against the castle, spun around, and exited the room to seek destruction elsewhere.

"And don't come back!" she shouted

as it turned the corner and rolled into the distance.

Snowpea hopped down to assess the damage. Nothing too bad: a couple of scratchers bumped out of place, a few blankets wrinkled. As she straightened everything back up, she could still feel her paws shaking.

Snowpea took a deep breath and exhaled slowly. "This is why I have to protect my land," she whispered to herself. "It can all be lost in an instant if I don't keep everything just right."

She hopped into bed, closed her eyes, and felt glad that at least her room was peaceful and clean again . . . for now.

CHAPTER 3

Puppy-nado

The next day, Snowpea munched on a bit of breakfast kibble, swept the crumbs from underneath her, licked her lips spotless, and looked to the doorway in anticipation of the fairy godmother.

"What gift do you have for me today?" she said with a grin, jumping up and down to try to get a glimpse as the human approached, cradling a large pillowy bed in her arms.

"A new bed?" Snowpea grinned. "You shouldn't have!"

But the bed began to whimper, and Snowpea looked up, trying to understand. Slowly, the fairy godmother lowered it to the ground, and to Snowpea's surprise, there were already two little sleeping furballs inside!

Is my gift . . . alive? she wondered.

What *were* they? They had black fur, wet noses, and floppy ears. They were just the same size as her, though they didn't look anything like her reflection. She leaned in to investigate the napping duo, her whiskers wiggling wildly as she took deep whiffs of their fur. She wasn't sure what to think, but she was sure she'd enjoy them, whatever—or whoever—they were!

"Maybe when they wake up, they'd like to help me tend to my garden . . . or have a tea party with me." She began to daydream quietly. "Oh, this will be just splendid!" Lying there curled up together, they looked so gentle and calm.

Suddenly, one of them began to yawn, which prompted the other to stretch, and it seemed they were both waking up.

Snowpea offered her paw to introduce herself. "How do you do? I'm Snowp—"

But faster than she could say her name, chaos broke loose.

"PUPPY-NADO!" one hollered, and jumped out of the bed, ripping through the room like a windstorm.

"PUPPY-NADO!" echoed the other, her big ears flopping up and down as she chased behind.

Snowpea's head bobbled wildly, trying to keep up as they ran in circles around her. Back and forth, side to side . . . they were zooming with no direction at all!

"Oh my! Could you please not—" Snowpea tried to interject as the puppies banged into the scratch posts, knocking them down.

Next, they galloped toward the windowsill, bumping into her beloved cat mint and smudging the glass with their slobbery snouts. "Mind the pots!" she cried as she caught the planter just before it hit the floor.

One puppy pulled a blanket off the cat bed and shook it between her teeth, growling.

The other ran over to the litter box and began digging enthusiastically, shoveling litter all over the floor. They were out of control!

Snowpea watched, stunned. Why would the fairy godmother bestow upon her this dreadful gift? Could they be returned?

The puppies slipped and slid on the tile, which was now covered in little sand-like grains, and once they caught their footing, they leapt up and pulled down Snowpea's brand-new glitter-wand.

"No!" Snowpea called out. "Not my wand!" But it was too late—the puppies were deep in a game of tug-of-war, fighting over her precious new toy as if it were a stick they'd found in the grass.

"Drop it!" Snowpea finally screamed loud enough to get their attention, and the wand fell to the floor as they opened their mouths in surprise. Had they not noticed her until now?

"Oh-em-gee, are you a new friend?!" shouted one puppy, her feet excitedly tapping the ground.

The other puppy ran over and planted a big, sloppy kiss on Snowpea's cheek. "NEW FRIEND!"

Snowpea rubbed her face with her paw, wiping away slimy puppy slobber. "Ick!"

The next thing she knew, the puppies were shoving their noses in the direction of her bum, sniffing wildly.

"That. Is. ENOUGH!" Snowpea screamed, her voice booming. Every hair on her body stood on end, making her look big and spiky. "That's quite enough!"

"Did we do something wrong?" said one puppy, her tail between her legs.

"You've done everything wrong! You've shown up and torn through my room like, like . . . monsters! And you *sniff my butt*? Have you no manners?"

"We were just trying to get to know you," said one pup.

Snowpea was aghast. "By *smelling my rump*?!"

The second pup lowered her head. "Isn't that how everyone introduces themselves?"

"*No!* I'll show you how you properly introduce yourself," Snowpea said, clearing her throat and extending her paw. "How do you do? I am Snowpea: Queen of Fosterland. I hail from the west—progeny of the great felids of the coastal sands. I am bound by fate to protect this glorious land and its bounty."

"Huh?" one pup whispered to the other.

"Um, I think she said she's from out-side," the pup whispered back.

"Precisely," Snowpea responded. "As a baby, I was all alone outdoors with nothing to my name. But I always knew I was bound for greater things—that one day I would be a queen." She shook the saliva off her glitter-wand and held it at her side. *"Queen Snowpea."*

"I'm Martha," said the wiry-haired pup. "My sister and I are from outside, too; we come from a long line of scruffy street dogs."

"And I'm Katharina, but you can call me Kat," said the pup with the long wavy fur. "Sorry to mess up your stuff. We were just trying to have a little fun. . . ."

"I see," Snowpea said, sighing. She stepped into the arched doorway of her castle and looked back at them. "Well, you may call yourself 'Kat,' but no feline would act that way. Now, please, leave me in peace. I've had enough excitement for today."

CHAPTER 4

Muddy Paws

After a brief catnap, Snowpea awoke to the blissful silence of Foster-land, and the puppies were nowhere in sight. She stretched her front legs out before her, then got to work cleaning up her room.

"I see you've got quite a mess on your paws," Haroun said from the door-way. Snowpea was embarrassed for him to see her space like this. Proper cats *don't* make messes!

"Oh, dear!" she peeped. "I can explain. It was these messy creatures who tore through the room—with no regard for feline decency!"

Haroun laughed. "That's puppies for ya! They sure know how to party. Don't you worry, puppies are generally simple creatures—eager to learn, easy to train. How are you coping with the new roommates?"

Snowpea's brows dropped. "*Roommates?* Haven't they gone away?"

Haroun pointed to the window. "They're probably just outside playing or getting puppy training. They're foster puppies—they live here in Foster-land for now. Just like you."

Snowpea stood on her hind limbs and peeked her nose over the windowsill. Sure enough, Kat and Martha were right outside, and they were running in circles through the dirt! With the back of her paw to her forehead, Snowpea fell backward, pretending to faint with all the drama she could muster, then opened one eye to check if Haroun was still pay-ing attention to her.

"Every cat needs to learn to play with others before they can go to their forever home. But I'll be honest . . . you and foster puppies? Even I didn't see that one coming." He chuckled.

Snowpea looked horrified.

"You'll be all right, kid," Haroun said, and continued on his way.

Snowpea sat in the window and watched the puppies zipping past, their tongues lashing wildly as they ran at warp speed. They seemed filled with pure joy, and for a moment she felt the corners of her lips curling into a smile as she watched them. But then—*splat!* A smattering of mud splashed against the window as they chased by, and Snowpea shook the grin off her face. Ugh! They were a mess!

Puppy training, she thought. *That's it! I can train them to have good manners. After all, I was here first—I make the rules.*

Soon, the puppies' energy seemed to wane, and they returned to the room exhausted, dragging their dirty paws on the floor. Snowpea's eye twitched at the brown prints that were now stamped across her room, but she took a deep breath and held her head high.

"Welcome back, puppies. We may have gotten off on the wrong . . . foot," she said, frowning at their dirty paws. "As the leader of this land, it is my duty to see that you are raised up right. And so, I'd like to extend to you an invitation to puppy school."

"Will there be treats?" asked Martha, with her tongue sticking out.

"Will there be toys?" asked Kat, with her feet tapping at the floor.

"You'll receive lessons in the proper usage of toys and treats, surely."

The puppies wagged their tails, and Snowpea smiled. It seemed they really were eager to learn!

"Well, then," Snowpea said. "The classes shall commence tomorrow!"

CHAPTER 5

Proper Puppy School

The next day, Snowpea stood with her wand at her side and her head held high. She was ready to teach the puppies to abide by her rules!

"Ahem!" she began. "Queen Snowpea's Proper Puppy School is officially in session." The puppies sat side by side, their butts wiggling eagerly. *Puppies are generally simple creatures, eager to learn*, Snowpea remembered, and took a deep breath, hoping it was true.

"Now, if we're going to get you two into tip-top shape, we're going to have to start with a baseline. First, I will assess how you drink water. Let's begin."

The puppies walked up to the bowl and began sloshing the water all around with their big tongues. *Gulp, gulp, gulp!* Water spilled out of the bowl, wetting the floor around them.

"Ugh, no! Here, watch me," she said, mopping the floor with a nearby blanket. She twinkled her toe beans and explained that the proper way to drink is to dip your paw into the

water, bring it to your face, and lick each droplet one at a time.

The puppies tilted their heads, con-fused. "That seems like a really ineffi-cient system," Martha noted. "But we'll try it. . . ."

After the puppies tried their best to impersonate Snowpea's paw work and managed to get only a few drops of water on the floor, Snowpea brought out three bowls of wet food. "Now we'll try it with food." Snowpea dipped her paw into the dish and curled her claws around a small bite-sized shred of meat, then brought it to her face and took a nibble. "Try to really savor each morsel. Simply delicious."

The puppies stared at Snowpea for a moment, then shoved their faces into their dishes and began to chow down.

"Manners!" Snowpea shouted, twinkling her paws at them as a reminder. "Mind your manners."

Martha furrowed her brow. "Can I be honest with you? This doesn't make a lot of sense to me. The less time it takes for food to get into your mouth, the better, right?" Kat nodded. "I mean . . . my mouth is *right here*."

Snowpea thought for a moment, then explained, "It's a matter of politeness. Just try."

Next up, it was time to teach them to play tetherball. She batted at the fluffy poof that dangled from a string atop one of her scratchers. "Give it a good tap with your paws, and it'll swing right back at you. It's a great way to build paw-eye coordination!"

Kat jumped up, grabbed the ball

between her teeth, and began to tug. Soon, the scratcher tipped over, and she was pulling the entire thing with her across the room. "I admire your strength," Snowpea grumbled as she pushed the post back into its rightful place, "but no—that's not it. Try again."

After a few more rounds of tetherball, Snowpea pulled out her toy basket hesitantly. She wasn't sure if she could trust the puppies with her toys, but they had to learn somehow. "I'm going to show you some of my toys now, and we're going to play the cleanup game."

"Toys? I love toys!" Martha smiled.

"Games? I love games!" Kat squealed.

"Well, hopefully you'll love this . . .

game. Whoever can put away the toys the fastest wins. Okay?" Snowpea dumped the toys onto the floor, then placed one back into the basket gently. "Like this. Now you try!"

Kat and Martha sniffed at the toys with curiosity but were quickly reminded to stay on task. One by one, they lifted each toy between their teeth and dropped them into the basket. Snowpea was delighted to see they really enjoyed fetching the items and putting them in their place! That is, until Kat went to pick up a little stuffed banana . . . and it squeaked.

Martha's ears shot up as Kat chewed on the toy. *Squeak, squeak!* The sound was irresistible! Martha grabbed hold of the other side of the banana, and the two of them spun in a circle, chewing and squeaking to their hearts' content.

"This banana is the best thing ever!" Martha squealed.

"Can we keep this one?" Kat begged, panting.

Snowpea sighed again. It was not easy to keep the puppies on task! Although, she did have to admit that their enthusiasm was kind of sweet, and for a moment she wondered if it might be fun to play with the toy, too. But now wasn't the time for that—she had to set a good example for them! She took a deep breath, then chimed in: "As long as you follow the rules, we'll be sure to schedule some toy time. For now, let's get back to class. This room isn't going to clean itself, and we can *never* leave toys scattered on the floor."

"Yes, Your Majesty," the puppies replied, and dropped the banana into the basket.

Finally, it came time for Snowpea to address something that had been bothering her ever since they'd arrived. She tapped them on their backs to prompt them to sit, then stood before them.

"This next subject might be . . . a sensitive matter," Snowpea said, trying her best not to be awkward. "I'm not going to name any names . . . but I've noticed that sometimes, *someone* seems to be going potty on the pad on the floor. If I can be honest with you, it's a little rude. A bathroom should be a place where you can cover your waste," she explained. She walked over to their poopy pad and frowned, trying to flip it in half.

The puppies listened intently.

"After going potty, you have to dig your paws through sand and cover everything up so that you've left no trace behind." She ran her paw through the litter to demonstrate. "You see? Better to use the litter box."

Martha's nose wrinkled. "Wait a minute. . . . That's *cat poop*? I thought those were free cookies!"

"I did, too!" admitted Kat, making a yucky face.

Snowpea grimaced. Maybe this was going to be harder than she thought.

CHAPTER 6

It's About Who

Over the days that followed, Snow-pea made a routine with the puppies that involved training, cleaning, and, as promised—just a bit of play. After lunch, Kat and Martha would lick their muzzles clean, and then Snow-pea would inspect their snouts for any smudges of food. "All clear!" she'd say if their fur was smooth and neat, which was their cue that they could have five minutes of toy time as a reward. And they always chose the same toy: the banana!

Squeak! Squeak! The puppies spun in a circle as they each held one end of the chew toy in their slobbery mouths. Snowpea sat in her cat castle, staring out the window, counting down the seconds until the squeaking would stop.

"Okay, time's up! Please deposit your toy into the basket," Snowpea said as a sunbeam slipped onto the castle. "We are now moving into sunshine meditation hour, and your silence is both appreciated and required." After ensuring that Martha had dropped the toy into the basket, Snowpea closed her eyes and soaked in the warmth of the golden light as it shined through the window.

But as she tried to slip into meditation mode, Snowpea's ear repeatedly tilted toward the puppies. She cracked open one curious eye and was surprised to find that they were still play-fighting. Spinning silently, their mouths hung open as they goofily bit at the air, making not a single sound aside from the clicking of their claws against the tile.

"Ahem," she said. "Toy time is over. What exactly are you two playing with?"

Kat smiled. "Imaginary banana."

Snowpea's face scrunched up, but as she looked down from her tower, she couldn't help but giggle at their make-believe. "Might I ask: How is it possible to play with a nonexistent toy?"

Martha dropped the imaginary banana. "Well . . . to play and have fun, you don't really need a toy. You only need a friend."

"Pals are way more important than stuff," Kat agreed.

Snowpea looked down at her paws. She'd had plenty of toys in her life, but she'd never really had a friend.

Kat continued. "We never had toys when we lived on the street, but we always had each other. The banana is awesome, but it's just a bonus."

Snowpea thought back to her first toy and said, "I didn't have toys on the street either. But when I arrived here, I was given the most beautiful sparkle-mouse! I'll never forget how much I loved that toy. . . ."

"But I've never seen a sparkle-mouse in the basket," Martha replied. "Where did it go?"

Snowpea felt her heart thump. She couldn't bring herself to tell them about the evil robot monster and how she lost her toy by leaving a mess on the floor. She had a reputation to keep as the tidy one! She looked out the window and said, "It's a long story."

The puppies gazed at Snowpea posted up in her palace.

"Think fast!" Kat suddenly hollered, and tossed an imaginary toy up to Snowpea. "Imaginary sparkle-mouse!"

Snowpea's pupils grew large, and in an instant, she clapped her paws together around the spot where the toy would have landed. Her head bobbled playfully, and her paws bopped at nothing, until she quickly remembered that there was no toy.

"Aha, you got me!" She winked. "Good one."

Kat winked back. "It's about *who* you play with—not *what* you play with!"

CHAPTER 7

Puppy Love

Snowpea found that, against the odds, she was starting to take a liking to the pups . . . that is, as long as they abided by her rules. They had learned not to cover the room with toys, having been trained to put everything away. They no longer sloshed water all over the floor as they slurped, having been trained to drink politely. And they certainly didn't continue eating the "free cookies" or digging through the sand—they knew it wouldn't please their feline leader one bit.

Out in the yard, it seemed that the fairy godmother was busy training them, too, and Snowpea watched as they learned new tricks. The human said a magical word, and it prompted the puppies to sit in the grass or to bow with their tails wagging eagerly. In a high-pitched tone, the godmother praised their performance, then gave them each a treat.

As she watched Martha and Kat learn to shake paws, Snowpea found herself cheering through the window.

Oh, what a difference they'd made since their butt-sniffing introductions!

In their attempt to avoid any mud puddles, the puppies walked instead of running, careful never to pick up too much speed. While Snowpea could see that they were holding back, she appreciated knowing that they'd return to the room with pristine paws.

It seemed that they were finally becoming the puppy princesses she wanted them to be and that everything in Fosterland was going *just right*.

But then Snowpea heard a sound in the distance.

Vrrr.

"No!" she cried, fearing that the

robot monster was heading in her direction. She looked to the doorway, and sure enough, the monster was rolling into view! Snowpea wished that the

puppies were there and that she didn't have to be alone and afraid.

With her paws over her mouth, she watched as the monster rolled past the door . . . and continued on to a different part of the house. *Phew.* It seemed that it wouldn't be visiting her bedroom this time.

Snowpea was trembling. She crept toward the doorway to ensure that the coast was clear, and as the whirring sound disappeared, it was replaced by the clicking of puppy claws coming down the hallway.

"Kat! Martha! Boy, am I glad to see you!" Snowpea admitted, and gave them each a big hug.

"Really?" Kat smiled, surprised by Snowpea's sudden affection.

"Really!" Snowpea said. "Hey, how about we have a slumber party tonight?"

Martha couldn't believe her ears. "You mean it? But you always curl up alone on top of your castle."

"Well . . . maybe it's about *who* you cuddle with, not *where you cuddle*," Snowpea said, crossing her toe beans in hopes that the puppies would say yes.

Kat and Martha nodded, jumping on their bed, leaving just enough room for Snowpea in between them. Snow-pea leapt into the soft plushness and felt herself disappearing into a puddle of puppy love. She had never felt so safe and warm in all her life! As she melted into a deep slumber, her purrs soothed the puppies both to sleep.

CHAPTER 8

Let's Throw a Ball

The next morning, Snowpea sat up in the giant dog bed and made an announcement: "Kat, Martha, I dare say you've learned to live like proper puppy princesses. And to reward you . . . I'm throwing you a ball!"

Martha's ears shot straight into the air. "Really? I thought you'd never say that!"

Kat zipped out of bed and ran across the room. "Throw it! Throw! Throw! Throw the ball!"

Snowpea giggled. "No, sillies. I'm not throwing you a *real ball*. I mean I'm going to organize, like, a fancy dinner party. A celebration!"

Martha looked at her feet. "Oh. Less exciting," she mumbled under her breath, while Kat slinked back over toward her sister.

"Don't be so mopey," Snowpea said. "It'll be fun! You can show off your new manners! We'll have food and drinks, and all the fanciest guests will be there—the foreign dignitaries from the Three-Cat Kingdom you've surely seen from the hall. We'll throw a party fit for royalty and show everyone that we're ready to rule."

Martha and Kat didn't seem very excited, but they agreed nonetheless.

Snowpea poked her head into the hallway—the border between Fosterland and the Three-Cat Kingdom. She cleared her throat and announced: "Hear ye, hear ye. I cordially invite each of you to the Fosterland Ball. This evening, just after sunset, we shall dance and dine. Two commonwealths joined as one!"

Haroun meowed from across the house. "Did you say dine? Count us in!"

Snowpea was elated. Finally, a

chance to show off and prove that the residents of Fosterland were dignified, regal, and worthy of one day expanding their reign beyond the bounds of their humble foster room.

All day long, Snowpea prepped and primped.

Kat and Martha watched as she swept around the litter box with her tail and washed the windows with baby wipes to remove the puppy-nose marks. "Everything has to be perfectly perfect!" Snowpea said as she rolled out a long red blanket in the doorway. "When they enter, they'll be so impressed!"

She put several crinkle balls along

a string and strung it between the tall cat towers on each side of the room. "A festive decoration." She smiled and stood back to admire her work.

After scooting boxes of cat food to the center of the room, she lined them all up in a row before covering the boxes in a long floral blanket. "This will be our dinner table—where we'll have our feast!"

She pulled three stuffed pumpkins out of a bin and arranged them nicely around the table, then laid out the table settings of dishes and little cloth napkins. Everything was coming together!

Looking in the mirror, she straightened her whiskers and groomed her paws until each toe bean was spotless and each claw shiny and white. Then she looked at the puppies and sighed.

"Let's get you girls ready for the ball," she said in a chipper voice, and began to comb through Martha's wiry, untamable mane with her paws. "Hmm. Just a little lick should slick this back nicely," she said, and saturated her fur in saliva as she forced Martha's curly locks into a puppy pompadour.

"Kat, let's not arrive at dinner with leftovers still crusted on our muzzle-puffs," she said as she spit-shined Kat's cheek.

Once the puppies were soaked from

grooming, they sat side by side and awaited direction. "Don't you think this is all a little silly?" Martha whispered to Kat. "All the formality?"

Kat whispered back, "I've never understood it either. . . . I'd much rather chase a ball than throw one." But Snowpea pretended not to hear—nothing would ruin today!

They sat like good little dogs and performed each task as Snowpea had them practice sitting, bowing, and, most importantly, shaking paws.

"Now, remember," Snowpea said as she extended her paw, "when you greet the cats, you offer your paw, and what do you say?"

"How do you do?" the puppies responded in unison.

"Very good!" Snowpea squealed. Through the window, she could see that the sky was pink and orange as the sun began to set. She patted the pups on the head and skipped to the doorway, inhaled deeply, and opened the door. "Let's make this a perfect evening, my puppy princesses!"

CHAPTER 9

Life of the Party

As the guests began to arrive, Snowpea and the puppies lined up at the door to greet them.

First came Coco, a sleek panther with shiny black fur and yellow-green eyes. She was the most senior leader of her kingdom, and Snowpea desperately longed for her approval.

"Welcome, Your Highness," Snowpea said as she and the puppies bowed.

Next came Eloise, a beautiful cat with a snow-white coat and one wise yellow eye. Snowpea curtsied, and the puppies extended their paws.

Last came Haroun. As the puppies offered him their greeting, he turned to Snowpea and smirked. "You really have trained them, haven't you?"

"Oh yes!" Snowpea said. "My reign in Fosterland has been quite a success, as I'm sure you'll see throughout the course of the night. Now, let me show you to your seats at the dinner table...."
Snowpea had pulled together a fancy menu from items in the Fosterland pantry, and as the hungry guests sat

in their assigned seats, she described each dish in detail.

"Welcome, guests! I have prepared a grand feast to celebrate this evening. As an appetizer, we have a light salad of organic, garden-fresh catnip with shaved bonito flakes. For our entrée, I've prepared a smear of savory pâté

topped with a sprig of locally grown cat grass. For our final course, a kibble pudding soaked in an aromatic gravy for the cats, and for the puppies, a very special bone-shaped biscuit-cake topped with a dollop of mashed legume. . . ."

Kat's and Martha's mouths began to

water. "I'm pretty sure that means pea-nut butter," Martha said excitedly.

"And to drink," Snowpea finished, "I've made us each a delectable *sardini martini*. Cheers to a perfect night!"

"Cheers!" said the guests.

Katharina took one lick of the bonito-flake salad, and the fishy flavor was so enticing that she swallowed it whole. Snowpea shot her a stern look as she licked her lips, and Kat whimpered.

Martha tried her best to eat one small piece at a time, but her appetizer and main course quickly vanished. Fortunately, the guests seemed focused on their own meals and unbothered by the puppies' poor manners.

"If I may," Snowpea began, wanting to strike up a polite conversation and distract from the puppies. "I'd love to hear about your experience ruling over such a vast territory. Thus far, we only know of life in this small foster room."

Coco licked the pâté from her lips and began. "Our forever home is a lovely one, with many rooms over which we are fortunate to rule. It's a great privilege to have visitors of many species pass by our borders." She looked at the puppies and smiled. "Of course, it is the ultimate journey for each of you little fosters to someday have your own forever home—your own Foreverland. All in due time!"

Snowpea nodded. "A great honor it will be to discover our future Foreverlands! And we've been practicing our royal ways, haven't we?" The puppies nodded, drooling as they eyed dessert.

"But remember," Coco cautioned, "Fosterland isn't just where you strive to find your home—it's where you strive to find *yourself*. So cherish these youthful moments of friendship and self-discovery, stay true to who you are, and most importantly: don't take life too seriously. You've got the rest of your life to be grown."

The puppies listened to her words of wisdom, their tails wagging. Taking her advice, Kat scooped a bit of peanut butter under her claw and flung it at her sister. *Splat!* It hit Martha on the nose, and she began licking the sweet treat over and over.

Kat checked on Coco's face, which had cracked a small smile, then looked back at her sister. "You look so silly." Kat laughed, and Martha flung peanut butter back at her until both of them were licking away.

"Um, puppies?" Snowpea's voice shook as she tried to smooth things over. "Food is for eating, not playing. . . ."

They licked and licked and licked, their tongues seeming to be stuck in the "on" position, and the more they licked, the more they started to laugh.

Eloise giggled quietly, and Haroun let out a tiny chuckle. Coco's face bore a soft grin, and again she said, "Cherish these moments!"

"But this isn't funny," Snowpea said as more peanut butter went flying, and the cats' laughs got louder. "This isn't how we behave! Knock it off!"

But it was too late—the puppies were having a giggle fit, and she had lost all control of them. Soon a food fight had broken out between Martha and Kat, who were tossing bits of biscuit into the air and flying upward to catch them, slam-dunking their desserts into their gaping mouths with all the enthusiasm of professional athletes. And worst of all, the cats were laughing heartily at the wild little puppies!

"Ain't no party like a puppy party. . . ." Eloise guffawed, and her feline friends agreed.

"We've seen many a messy foster puppy, but these two really *take the cake*!" Haroun cracked himself up.

The more the cats laughed, the more wound-up the puppies became. They jumped onto the table, stepping into unfinished dishes and leaving a trail of wet paw prints behind them. Martha held a stuffed pumpkin between her teeth and growled, tempting Kat to tug at the other side. Soon, the pumpkin was destroyed, and the entire table was covered in fluffy white stuffing.

."Lovely, it's snowing," Coco joked. She was well used to the destructive-ness of puppies and could laugh it off— but Snowpea didn't think it was funny whatsoever. She was mortified.

"Cut it out! You're being bananas!" Snowpea cried, and quickly realized she had said a word she should never have uttered.

"BANANA!" Kat screamed, and they leapt over the table, knocking over the sardini martinis to retrieve the stuffed banana from the toy bin. *Squeak, squeak, squeak!* The toy cheeped as they tugged it back and forth, growling

and bumping into Snowpea's cherished décor.

"Sit!" Snowpea screamed, but her commands couldn't be heard over the squeaking of the banana. "Bow!" she cried, but her orders were useless— the puppies were too engrossed in their shenanigans to pay any attention to her.

Squeak, squeak, squeak!

She held her head in her paws and began to weep.

There was no going back. They'd broken into a full-on puppy-nado, zooming in circles, and the three cats seemed to take that as their cue to leave. They thanked Snowpea for an entertaining night, and just like that, they were gone.

Standing in the eye of a puppy hurricane, dishes scattered throughout the room and pâté smeared against the walls, Snowpea opened her mouth and let out a cry: "YOU RUINED MY PARTY!"

CHAPTER 10

Drawing a Line

Huffing and puffing, Snowpea could feel a rage spilling over her like a sardini martini on a floral tablecloth. She slammed the door shut and said:

"Look at you! Look at what you've done! You ruined everything! Are you descended from wolves?!"

Kat held her tail between her legs,

ashamed. Martha scratched her head, pondering the question.

"I trusted you! I thought you had learned how to be neat and polite. But it turns out the only thing you know how to clean . . . is your plates!" The puppies licked their chops; she wasn't wrong. Snowpea broke down in tears. "I haven't cried like this since I lost my sparkle-mouse." She wiped her face with her paws, but the tears kept falling.

"Please don't cry, Snowpea," Kat said earnestly.

"Coco said not to take things so seriously, and, well . . ." Martha looked at the plates scattered on the floor. "We just got carried away."

"Self-discipline is a virtue, you know!" Snowpea wailed.

"But so is self-expression, right?" Martha tilted her head.

Snowpea grumbled. The pup had a point, but it wasn't a point she wanted to take.

"You know what? Fine! Express your-selves all you want . . . on *your* side of the room. This is where I draw the line. This land is hereby divided into two!"

She began hanging blankets from the strings she'd hung, making a border down the center of the foster room. One blanket at a time, she banished the puppies from her side of Foster-land. She pushed all of the mess to their side of the line, quickly scrubbed her side clean, tossed over their bed, and screamed, "Stay out of my room!" before hanging one final blanket on the line and shutting herself in.

The puppies felt terrible. Now that they were left to clean up their own

mess, they realized they may have taken their shenanigans *a little* too far. They stood surrounded by fluff and food and scattered dishes and toys, unsure of where to start with cleaning up. But worst of all, they'd disappointed Snowpea and lost their friend.

"What should we do?" asked Kat. She started to place the toys in the basket and tried to remember how Snowpea had taught her to scrub the floor.

Martha stacked the dishes and wiped the walls. "All we can do is clean up our mess . . . and hope Snowpea can forgive us."

"The thing is, I never quite understood the point of having a squeak toy if you can't squeak it whenever you want . . . ," Kat admitted.

". . . Or a mud puddle if you can't run through it! I know, I really get it," Martha agreed. "But maybe there's room for compromise. Maybe there's a time and a place to be a party pup."

"*At a party*, I thought," Kat said, scrubbing the floor. "Although, we probably didn't need to dance on the table and knock over everyone's food, now that I think about it. . . ."

They stayed up cleaning until the room was spotless, and just before hopping into bed, they looked at the newly erected blanket wall that now divided them from their feline friend.

"How can we show her we're sorry? She loves gifts. Should we leave her a gift?" Martha asked.

Kat walked over to the basket and picked up their favorite banana toy. It was their most beloved item . . . but it had caused them such trouble. "Let's give her the banana. Hopefully when she sees our peace offering, she'll accept our apology." The two puppies slipped the banana halfway under the blanket and hopped into bed, hopeful for what the next day would bring.

CHAPTER 11

Learning the Hard Way

The next morning, Snowpea awoke in her castle all alone. She hadn't heard what the puppies had been up to on the other side of the curtain barrier the night before, but she figured they'd probably been rolling in the garbage . . . or pooping on the floor! It had been the worst night of her life, and she couldn't believe she ever thought the puppies could really be her friends.

Now Fosterland was silent, and her blanket was blocking her view of the messy pup-side of the room. She stretched, rubbed her puffy eyes, and looked out the window. With no puppies around, the room felt cold and empty.

Maybe solitude is the best thing for me, she thought. *Maybe I was always meant to be my own best friend—to be a ruler of one.* As she gazed out the window, she saw that the puppies were prancing out to play and quickly looked away. If they wanted to run in the mud or drag dirt around their side of the room, well then, that was their problem to mop up. "All I can do is keep my side of the room clean. . . ."

She looked at the partition and noticed that half of the banana toy was sticking into her section. ". . . Which is more than those puppies can say! Seems like they can't even manage to

keep the mess on their side of the line," she moaned, and kicked the toy back underneath. "I bet it's a disaster on their side!"

Suddenly, she heard a distant hum, which was slowly getting louder.

Vrrrrr.

"Oh no!" she said, looking side to side and quickly scurrying back to the top of the castle.

The small robotic machine clanged and clamored as it made its way into the room, terrorizing her with every whirr of its wheels. "I have nothing for you!" she screamed, looking around her side of the room, which was spotless. But as the robot slid around the puppies' half of the room, she realized that they were in for a rude awakening—anything they'd left lying around would soon vanish into the unforgiving mouth of the monster.

For a moment, she felt guilty knowing that the puppies were blissfully bounding in the grass and would soon come in to find that their belongings had been carried away. But she furrowed her brow and grumbled to herself: "I warned them to keep their room clean, didn't I? Well, then! Sometimes we all have to learn the hard way! Hmmph!"

The robot monster crashed around their side of the room, and soon she heard the squeak of the banana toy as it was consumed by the beast. *Squeak . . . squeak . . . squeaaaaaaak.* She closed her eyes and covered her ears as the robot trundled off into the distance. And although deep down she felt the sting of guilt, she let her anger get the best of her and said to herself: "No more squeaky banana. That'll teach them."

The next sound she heard was the tippy-tapping of puppy paws coming in from their playtime. Snowpea tiptoed over to the curtains and held her ear to the blanket, curious to hear their reaction.

"Look!" Martha said in a cheery tone. "The banana is gone!"

Snowpea scratched her head. Why did she seem *happy* to have lost the toy? Shouldn't she be upset?

Kat squealed. "Snowpea accepted our peace offering!"

Snowpea's heart sank into her gut. *Peace offering?*

"She took our gift! Maybe she still wants to be our friend!" Martha replied.

Snowpea couldn't believe what she was hearing. She lifted the curtain and poked her head through. ". . . Wait a minute. The banana was a gift . . . for me? But that's your favorite toy."

The puppies ran to meet her. "Snowpea! We wanted you to have it. You mean more to us than any toy ever could! We are so sorry we ruined your party. Can you forgive us?"

Snowpea began to cry. "Yes . . . but I'm not sure I can forgive myself."

CHAPTER 12

The Tale of the Toy Thief

Snowpea felt horrible. By trying to teach the dogs a lesson, she'd caused the same thing to happen to them that had happened to her as a baby. Only this time it was worse, because she'd known exactly what would happen.

She lowered her head. "It's time for me to tell you about the toy thief," she confessed. The puppies sat with their heads tilted in curiosity.

"Do you remember how I told you about my first toy? When I was just a tiny kitten, I had a sparkle-mouse that glittered in the light, with green ears and a satin tail that dangled behind it. This toy was the first gift I was ever given. . . . It meant everything to me. I would chase it all over the room, and it brought me pure happiness."

The puppies listened carefully.

"But then one day, I heard a sound. A high-pitched buzz that grew louder and louder until it was all I could hear! And then . . . I saw it. THE EVIL ROBOT MONSTER!"

Gasp! The puppies' ears shot up. "Evil robot monster?" Kat shrieked.

"Glowing eyes and a thick exterior shell, the monster zoomed straight toward my toy, and—VROOM! Just like that, my toy vanished into the unforgiving teeth of the beast. That was the last time I ever saw my precious sparkle-mouse," she said tearfully. "And now . . . it's taken your banana, and it's all my fault."

Martha wrapped her arm around Snowpea. "That sounds terrible."

Snowpea nodded, still ashamed. "I think . . . I think that's why I'm so particular about cleaning and manners. I thought if I kept everything

just right, bad things wouldn't happen anymore . . . and I wouldn't lose anything else that mattered to me." She felt a lump in her throat as she realized that the puppies were her most treasured gift of all . . . and she'd pushed them away. If Snowpea hadn't been so set on teaching them *her* way to do things, they could have been best friends by now.

"It's okay," said Kat. "Of course you would become a neat freak. Err—not a *freak*. A neat cat. What I mean is . . . of course you would value cleaning. I'm sorry we didn't fully understand that before."

Snowpea sniffled. "You guys are

too kind. I can't believe that I've let the monster run off with your favorite banana. I've got to make it right! How can I make this up to you?"

Kat and Martha sat and pondered. "Well, we could try to go get the banana back," Martha said.

"An adventure!" Kat squealed. "Three friends against the evil robot monster—it doesn't stand a chance!"

"I don't know. That could be really dangerous, and even messy," Snowpea worried. "Besides, who even knows where the monster's lair is? All I know is that it's somewhere beyond our border, in the Three-Cat Kingdom."

"So, let's go! We'll search for it and

we'll make it pay!" Martha said, and Kat's legs began to run in place, eager for the chase.

Snowpea sat up. She was through with living a clean, quiet, solitary life because of some monster who tried to scare her as a baby. It was time for her to stand up for herself and her friends! She stood tall and hollered at the top of her lungs: "Let's go get your banana!"

CHAPTER 13

Vac Attack

Snowpea, Martha, and Kat peered through the doorway of the foster room out into the Three-Cat Kingdom. Haroun was napping high up in a cat tree, while Coco and Eloise were perched in windows, fast asleep. "The coast is clear," Snowpea whispered. "Let's go find our monster."

They crept down the hallway, pausing to look in each room. The scent of dinner in the kitchen was enticing, and for a moment, the puppies seemed to float on air in its direction, but they quickly returned to Snowpea's side.

Way down at the other end of the house, a shadowy figure sat quietly in the corner. They tiptoed closer to investigate until Snowpea let out a small shriek: "Eep!"

It was the monster!

Kat placed a paw over Snowpea's mouth and quietly whispered: "It's okay. You'll be okay. We're all here together."

"It looks like he's asleep," Martha noted. "He isn't moving at all."

She was right. The monster looked completely unaware of their presence, seemingly deep in slumber. The three of them sniffed around his edges, smelling the musty scent of old dust that he'd sucked into his chambers over time.

"Maybe one of these buttons will release the banana," Martha suggested. But just as Snowpea reached out to stop her, Martha pushed a button atop his head, and suddenly . . .

VRRRRR!

The trio shot back, barking and hissing. The monster was awake!

With glowing red eyes and hungry spinning teeth for feet, the monster moved in their direction as they ran down the hallway, screaming at the top of their lungs.

"Grab the leash!" Martha yelled. "We can try to capture him!"

Snowpea frantically grabbed a leash off the wall and swung it over her head like a lasso, missing the robot entirely as it passed them by and nearly smacking Eloise in the butt.

"I'm sorry! It's just . . . well . . . no time

for explanations!" Snowpea hollered, galloping by as she and her puppy pack chased the speedy robot down the hall. Coco, Eloise, Haroun, and even the fairy godmother, who had rushed out of the kitchen to see what was happening, shook their heads at the chaos. But Snowpea didn't have time to worry about appearances. Right now, all that mattered was stopping the monster's destruction once and for all and getting back the banana toy for her friends!

"Hop on my back!" Kat yelled, and Snowpea mounted her like a cowgirl on a horse. They ran together at lightning speed, their fur blowing backward and their mouths agape, until they were close enough for Snowpea to swing the leash overhead and toss it at the robot with all her might. "Now—pull!" Kat screeched as it wrapped around the monster . . . but the monster quickly

zipped away, crashing into a wall and escaping into a side room.

Snowpea hopped off the pup, and the three of them peeked at the robot as it ate paperclips and rubber bands that had fallen from a desk. "It's eating everything in sight," she grumbled. "We have to jump on it and get it to stop!"

As the robot slid toward the door, the whirring sound was booming. Snowpea trembled, but she knew she had to pounce. "Rawr!" she screamed as she leapt on top of the robot, all four paws balancing on top of the gliding machine. The puppies howled and barked, chasing behind her as the robot took off underneath her feet, carrying her back down the hallway.

"Whoa-oa-oh!" Snowpea shrieked as the robot zoomed in a tight circle, spinning her like a ballerina. As the room whirled around her, she started to grin. *This is kind of fun*, she realized, and let out a loud "Woo-hoo!" until she flew off the robot's back.

The puppies huddled around the dizzy kitten as the monster slid into the foster room. "Are you okay?!" they asked.

"I'm good . . . I'm great. Okay, now—think, Snowpea, think!" she said as she steadied herself. She needed to focus. How could they retrieve the banana

and stop the robot monster from eating all their toys?

"Maybe," Martha said. "Maybe we need to feed it so much that it can't stomach another bite. If puppies know anything about food, it's that we won't ever stop eating it until we've had so much that it's physically impossible to continue."

"We do have impressive appetites," Kat agreed.

"That's brilliant!" Snowpea shouted, her imagination sparked. She hopped into the litter box and said, "Get in, girls! We've got sand to kick!" The three friends stood inside the litter box, kicking and digging as bits of litter flew all over the floor.

"I can dig this!" Martha quipped, burrowing her front legs into the litter and covering the room in tiny grains.

As the monster approached, the three stood in the empty plastic box and d as it sucked up the sand, seem-

o cough and choke. *Vrrr-ttt-tt-t.*

Vrrr-ttt-tt-t. The robot was struggling.

"I hope there's a cookie in there for you, too, you fiend!" Martha yelled. But now wasn't the time for jokes—now was the time to plot their final blow.

Snowpea looked up at the blankets hanging in the center of the room. They reminded her of the fight that had divided her from the puppies, and she wanted nothing more than to rip the barrier down. And then it hit her: "We can trap the monster under the blankets—like a net!"

The monster banged and clanged around the room, knocking into the toy basket and the scratch post, and each collision made Snowpea jump. But no monster could get away with stealing from her friends!

She climbed the scratcher and held on to one end of the string. Across the room, Kat and Martha leapt up toward the string. And on the count of three, just as the evil robot monster passed under the blankets, Snowpea yelled: "Tear down the blanket wall!"

Vrrrr–rrrr–rr–r–sppt–tt–t–t–trrrh–hhm. The robot sucked up the blankets until its mouth was jammed. And at long last, the monster machine spun fully onto its back and broke down completely.

At first, they were afraid to approach.

Snowpea observed from a distance, then grabbed her wand scepter and held it away from her body, poking at the upside-down monster to see if its little teeth-feet would move. But the room was silent and still, aside from the sound of puppies panting and drooling on the floor in exhaustion. "Did we do it?" Kat asked. "Did we slay the beast?"

Snowpea held her head up high and declared with pride: "Hear ye, hear ye. At long last the evil robot monster . . . has perished!" She tapped at the compartment on the bottom where the blankets had jammed its wicked jaws. "Now let's get your banana!"

Snowpea ripped the robot's bottom off, and inside she could see a vast collection of dust, cat fur, sand, bits of garbage, and . . . the banana toy! As she grabbed the filthy yellow toy, she shook it, and dust went flying through the air, making the room sparkle and the puppies sneeze.

"I can't believe . . . *achoo!* . . . you got our toy back!" Kat squealed. "You're a true friend. A true queen!"

"*Achoo!* A true queen!" Martha agreed, grabbing hold of the squeaky toy with Kat.

They *squeak-squeak-squeaked* and spun in circles, ears flopping and drool flying. The look of joy on their faces was contagious, and Snowpea could no longer hold back her happiness. "Life's too short not to have a little fun with your friends . . . and make a little mess!" she said, and she grabbed an armful of debris from the belly of the beast and tossed it into the air.

A cloud of dust and dirt surrounded her, and as she looked above her, paws in the air, she saw something sparkling overhead.

"It's my glitter-mouse!" she cried as her beloved childhood toy fell into her arms.

Snowpea darted around the filthy room, chasing her glitter-mouse with carefree bliss, and the puppies joined

in on the fun, too. For the rest of the afternoon, they took turns batting their toys around together and leaping over one another with unbridled joy. And although it was noisy—and although it was a mess—playing with her friends made life feel perfectly perfect.

CHAPTER 14

Bless This Mess

Weeks passed by, and Snowpea and the puppies had become closer than ever. Kat and Martha had learned to be playful without being (too) destructive, and Snowpea had learned that sometimes a *little* bit of chaos actually made life more fun . . . and that friendship was more important than anything you could own.

As the sun rose through the window of Fosterland, Snowpea awoke squeezed between the doggy duo, who were licking her cheeks with their huge tongues. She giggled, happy to receive love in the form of a morning bath. "It smells like puppy breath in here!" She laughed. "Thank you for that."

Haroun stepped into the doorway just as Snowpea's mane was sticking straight up, styled with saliva. "Nice hair." He smirked.

"That's puppies for ya!" Snowpea replied with a wink.

"Well, little ones, I came to tell you that today is a very special day," Haroun said. "It's the day you each find your home—the kingdom over which you shall forever reign." He bowed his head, then pointed to the window.

Snowpea, Martha, and Kat peeked through the glass to see that the fairy

godmother was setting up a large play-
pen in the grass, where each of them
would soon meet their adopters.

"Oh, I'm so excited to meet my
people!" Kat squealed. "When they
arrive, I'm going to bow and then offer
them my paw, like this," she said, lifting
a foot.

"Ooh! And don't forget to ask, 'How
do you do?'" Martha chimed in.

"Just be yourselves!" Snowpea
smiled. "They're going to love the two
of you *exactly* as you are." It was funny
for Snowpea to think that she tried to
put Kat and Martha through puppy
school . . . when it turned out that she
was the one with the most lessons to

learn. The friendship the three of them shared would stay with her forever.

Soon, the fairy godmother came to bring them outside, where they played in the grass and chased their favorite toys together while they awaited their adopters.

Kat's adopters were the first to arrive. They clipped a small harness on her, and she held her head high to show off for her friends. "Look at that! I'm ready for a life of hiking and playing! Do I look like a grown dog?"

"Oh, Kat, you look marvelous—like the Queen of the Mountaintop!" Snowpea smiled.

Then came Martha's adopter, who

tossed her a small tennis ball. "Look at me! I'm ready to play fetch at the beach! What do you think?" Martha said with pride.

"Martha, you'll be the Queen of the Shore!" Snowpea said.

Finally, after the puppies' adopters went inside to pack up Kat's and Martha's things, it was Snowpea's turn to meet her adopter, and she groomed herself in the sunshine to prepare for the most important introduction of her life. "Oh, I hope I make a good first impression," she said under her breath as her person approached with a basket of toys in her hand.

"Snowpea, you'll be the Queen of

Foreverland, and a fine friend to all who live there!" said Martha.

Kat nodded and booped Snowpea on the nose with her muddy paw.

Cross-eyed, Snowpea looked down at her nose and saw that it was now splotched with mud—right before she

was meeting her forever family. She looked up at the puppies and smiled. "Thank you! Hey, a little dirt never hurt!" She hugged her puppy friends tight one last time, then turned with her head held high, dirt smudge and all, to meet her adopter and finally head to her very own kingdom.

The True Story of Snowpea

Snowpea was found outside without a mother when she was just a day old and was brought to an animal shelter in Chula Vista, California. From there, she came to my house and was placed in a toasty incubator where she could be cozy and warm during her first weeks of life. As she grew up, I hoped that we would eventually be able to find another foster kitten to be her friend.

Around that time, a litter of new-born puppies was rescued from right across the border in Tijuana, Mexico, and they needed a safe place to go. My nonprofit organization, Orphan Kitten Club, divided the puppies into different foster homes (puppies are a lot of work!) and two of them—Martha and Katharina—came to stay with me! Since Snowpea didn't have any kitten friends, we decided to introduce her to the little puppies who were right around her size.

Snowpea was curious and friendly right away, and she loved to play with the puppies! But the one thing she didn't like was how messy they were while potty training. She was always trying to cover their stinky pee pads! Snowpea would groom them vigorously and always tried her best to keep them—and their room—clean. Over time, the puppies learned to go potty outside, and Snowpea loved them as if they were her sisters. Whenever the puppies slept in their dog bed, Snowpea would squish in between them as if she were a puppy, herself!

Martha and Katharina are now big, fluffy dogs who each found loving homes, and Snowpea is treated like a queen in a forever home of her own. The three of them just might be one of the cutest foster groups I have ever had!

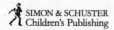

READ & LEARN

with

simon kids

Keep your child reading, learning,
and having fun with Simon Kids!

A one-stop shop where you can
**find downloadable resources, watch interactive author
videos, browse books by reading level, and more!**

Visit us at
SimonandSchusterPublishing.com/ReadandLearn/

And follow us @SimonKids

SIMON & SCHUSTER
Children's Publishing